Fact Finders®

It's Back to School ... Way Back!

School in
PIONEER
TIMES

by Kerry A. Graves

CAPSTONE PRESS
a capstone imprint

Fact Finder Books are published by Capstone Press,
1710 Roe Crest Drive, North Mankato, Minnesota 56003.
www.mycapstone.com

Library of Congress Cataloging-in-Publication Data
Names: Graves, Kerry A., author.
Title: School in pioneer times / by Kerry A. Graves.
Description: North Mankato, Minnesota: Capstone Press, 2017. |
Series: Fact finders. It's back to school ... way back! | Includes bibliographical references.
Identifiers: LCCN 2015048716| ISBN 9781515720966 (library binding)
ISBN 9781515721000 (paperback) | ISBN 9781515721048 (ebook pdf)
Subjects: LCSH: Education—United States—History—19th century—Juvenile literature. |
    Schools—United States—History—19th century—Juvenile literature. |
    Frontier and pioneer life—United States—Juvenile literature.
Classification: LCC LA206 .G73 2017 | DDC 370.973—dc23
LC record available at http://lccn.loc.gov/2015048716

Editorial Credits
Editor: Nikki Potts
Designer: Kayla Rossow
Media Researcher: Jo Miller
Production Specialist: Kathy McColley

Photo Credits
Alamy: eye35, 23; Bridgeman Images: Private Collection/Peter Newark American Pictures, 6; Getty
Images: Photoquest, cover, Underwood Archives, 13; Granger, NYC - All rights reserved., 19, 20, 22,
25, 27; Newscom: akg-images, 4, 7; North Wind Picture Archives, 11, 15, 21, 28; Shutterstock: Chris
H. Galbraith, 18, davidsansegundo, cover (background), Everett Historical, 5, Lagui, 29; Wikimedia:
Joefreeman83, 16; Design Elements: Shutterstock: Frank Rohde, iulias, marekuliasz, Undrey

Printed and bound in the USA.
009671F16

TABLE OF CONTENTS

Chapter 1

A NEW HOME IN THE WEST

In the 1800s people from the eastern states began settling the western territories of the United States. Some traveled to the modern-day states of Illinois, Wisconsin, Iowa, Minnesota, Nebraska, South Dakota, and North Dakota. They packed their belongings in covered wagons and hitched oxen, mules, or horses to the wagons to pull the load. Pioneers journeyed for several months across hundreds of miles of unsettled land.

A family stands in front of their wagon in Loup Valley, Nebraska in 1886.

a Western Missouri pioneer homestead in 1820

The U.S. government gave pioneers a piece of land. When they arrived at this land claim, pioneers had to build a home and farm buildings. Some families lived in their wagons or in tents until a permanent shelter could be built. In wooded areas pioneers cut down trees to build log homes. Men cut notches in the logs to fit them together. Then they filled gaps with a mud and grass mixture called chinking.

On the prairie pioneers built "soddys." They used a special plow to cut strips of dirt and grass from the prairie. They then cut the **sod** into blocks. The settlers stacked sod blocks on top of each other to build walls.

In some areas of the prairie pioneers dug their homes into the side of a hill. They stacked sod bricks in front of the dugout, making a wall that sealed the hole. They covered window openings with blankets or animal hides. This prevented cold winds and dust from blowing into their homes.

sod homestead in Custer County, Nebraska, 1887

sod—a layer of soil with grass attached to it

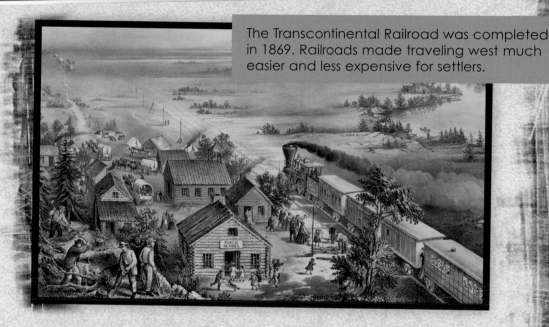

The Transcontinental Railroad was completed in 1869. Railroads made traveling west much easier and less expensive for settlers.

Few towns existed on the western frontier during the early 1800s. Most supplies had to be made by hand rather than purchased. Pioneers crafted their own furniture, clothes, butter, candles, and soap.

As the railroads extended to the west, many pioneers rushed to the Midwest to build homes. As frontier settlements grew, towns were formed. People opened general stores, bakeries, post offices, lumber mills, and schools.

MAP OF THE WESTERN FRONTIER, LATE 1800s

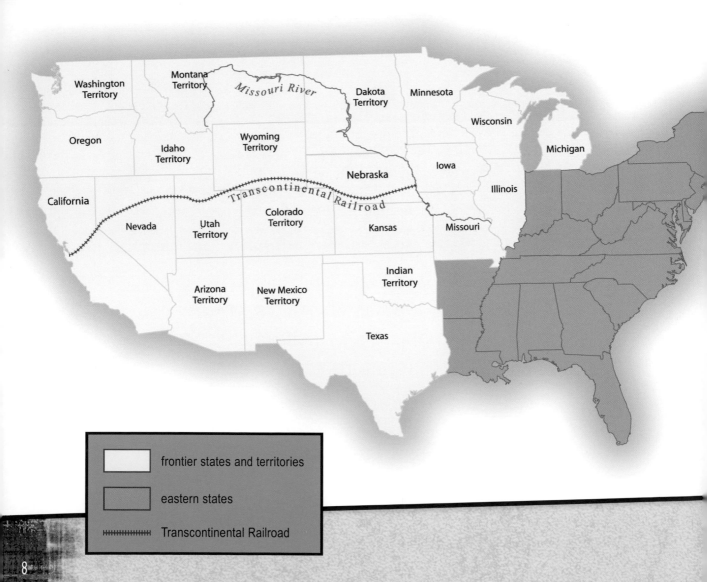

Washington Territory

Montana Territory

Missouri River

Dakota Territory

Minnesota

Wisconsin

Oregon

Idaho Territory

Wyoming Territory

Iowa

Michigan

Nebraska

Illinois

California

Nevada

Utah Territory

Colorado Territory

Kansas

Missouri

Transcontinental Railroad

Arizona Territory

New Mexico Territory

Indian Territory

Texas

frontier states and territories

eastern states

Transcontinental Railroad

8

The Frontier

In the 1800s pioneers called unsettled territories of the western United States the frontier. It stretched from the Missouri River to the California coast.

The U.S. government divided the frontier into territories and passed laws to encourage people to move there. Congress passed the Townsite Act in 1844. The law allowed people to buy 320 acres of land for $1.25 per acre. Later the government offered **veterans** of the Mexican War (1846–1848) and the Civil War (1861–1865) free land in honor of their military service.

The Homestead Act of 1862 gave 160 acres of free land to people who were interested in building homes and farms west of the Missouri River. Thousands of people traveled in wagon trains across the plains, prairies, and mountains to help settle the West. However, much of this land was American Indian territory. As the settlers claimed land in the West, American Indians were moved to **reservations** by the government. The reservations were much smaller than where tribes originally lived. Life became very hard for native peoples.

veteran—a person who served in the armed forces
reservation—an area of land set aside for American Indians; in Canada reservations are called reserves

Farming the land was difficult. The prairie sod had to be broken up before crops could be planted. Early settlers used axes and simple plows to dig up the sod. The farmers became known as "sodbusters."

Settlers suffered through many **hardships**. Temperatures could reach more than 100 degrees Fahrenheit during summer and drop below 0°F during winter. **Droughts**, heavy rains, hail, or an early frost sometimes damaged crops. Strong winds blew clouds of dust into the air, making it hard for farmers to see while working in the fields. During blizzards snow blew thickly. Pioneers sometimes tied ropes between the house and the barn, allowing them to find their way to the animals and back to the house.

hardship—something that causes suffering; usually hunger and poverty

drought—a long period of weather with little or no rainfall

Families worked together to farm the land. Each family member had assigned chores to finish every day. Women and girls started cooking fires early in the morning while men and boys gathered their tools and hitched the oxen to plows.

Some pioneer children went to school during the day and finished their chores when they returned home. Pioneer women spent the day baking, sewing, and washing clothes. Many women and girls also helped with planting and harvesting. Children helped feed the farm animals, milk the cows, gather eggs, churn butter, and weed the garden.

A mother and her children prepare a meal and gather wood near their log cabin in the 1800s.

Chapter 2

SCHOOLING ON THE WESTERN FRONTIER

The main goal of frontier schools was to teach children to read and write. Most parents wanted their children to be able to read the Bible. Some pioneer families wanted their children to learn arithmetic. These families often operated businesses in frontier towns. **Immigrant** families relied on schools to teach their children English.

Most frontier schools held classes from mid-November to April, after the fall harvest and before the spring planting. But the schoolhouse was open whenever a teacher could be found. Sometimes this meant holding school sessions during summer. Children only attended when class did not interfere with farm chores. Many children quit school after they learned to read.

immigrant—someone who moves from one country to live permanently in another

A teacher stands with her students of various ages outside of a country schoolhouse in the late 1880s or early 1890s.

The pioneer community supported the schoolteacher. Parents paid **tuition** for each child. The fees averaged $1 to $3 per student. Tuition rates varied depending on how long the child stayed in school and what subjects he or she studied. Some children did chores at the school in exchange for lessons.

Most schools taught students who ranged in age from 4 to 21. Schoolchildren of all ages often studied in a single classroom. Class sizes varied depending on the season and number of families in the area.

tuition—money paid to attend a school

Pioneer Schoolteachers

Many teachers in the early 1800s had limited training as educators. Most teachers were young men or women who had completed a full course of schooling. The teacher often was only 16 or 17 years old.

By the late 1800s farms and towns were firmly established. Children had more time for school. And parents wanted teachers to have more training. Eleven normal schools had opened on the East Coast by the year 1860. The schools offered a two-year training program for teachers.

Some teachers traveled from the East to take jobs on the frontier. But convincing teachers to travel to frontier towns was difficult. Most pioneer communities could not afford to pay schoolteachers much money. Many teachers made only $10 to $35 a month.

Some teachers found rooms to rent at boarding houses. Many teachers had to "board around" with the families of their students. They lived and ate meals with a pioneer family and moved to a different home every few weeks.

A boy stands in front of his teacher for his reading lesson.

Most frontier schools did not have specific grades like schools in the eastern cities. Children progressed through various levels of readers, spellers, and arithmetic as fast as they could. This depended on how often they could attend. Once they mastered a subject, children advanced to more difficult topics.

Students in frontier schools often worked independently. The teacher met with small groups of students throughout the day. Teachers expected the rest of the students to study quietly until their group's turn.

Early frontier schools did not have writing paper. Most schools could not afford paper and ink supplies. Students wrote arithmetic problems and spelling words on boards made of **slate**. Instead of pens students used slate pencils or chalk. After the teacher reviewed the assignment, children erased their work with a damp cloth. Students were able to use the slates over and over again.

slate—gray rock that can be split into thin layers

Chapter 3

PIONEER SCHOOLHOUSES

Many frontier farms were scattered across the prairie. Pioneers built the schoolhouse in a central location. Some schoolhouses were made from sod. But in other areas each family **donated** wood to use for building the school. Everyone helped "raise" the school. The building event brought members of a community together.

a rural schoolhouse in Waterloo, Iowa

donate—to give something as a gift

The schoolhouse usually was a large rectangular building with windows along the sides. Some schools had a small entryway for hanging coats and hats. In most schoolhouses one or more blackboards covered the wall behind the teacher's desk. Most schoolhouses had a space above the blackboard for hanging writing examples or artwork. The teacher's desk sometimes was set on a raised platform. It gave the teacher a good view of the room.

Seating arrangements varied from school to school. In some schools desks lined the side walls. Students often sat on long benches at the desks. Other schools had rows of student benches or individual desks that faced the teacher. The youngest children sat in the front desks. The older students sat at the back of the classroom. Many teachers separated the boys and girls. Girls sat on one side of the room and the boys sat on the opposite side.

FACT

Schoolhouses had many purposes. Teachers used them for recitals and examinations. In some areas the building served as a school during the week, a church on Sunday, and a place for community meetings.

Indoor plumbing did not exist yet. The teacher kept a water bucket next to the front or rear entrance. Thirsty children used a dipper to scoop water from the bucket. Some schoolhouses had a well nearby where they drew water. If the schoolhouse did not have a well, children often took turns filling the water bucket at a nearby stream. Children used outhouses behind the schoolhouse when they had to go to the toilet.

a simple, one-room schoolhouse in Nevada City, Montana

A teacher addresses his students.

Keeping Order in the Schoolhouse

Teachers were expected to teach good **morals** to their students. They punished students for tardiness, speaking out of turn, fighting, or causing other disruptions. Schools wanted teachers who were good at "lickin" as well as learnin.

Schoolteachers sometimes were strict. Many teachers disciplined disobedient students with a ruler or a small tree branch. They sometimes locked the children in a closet. Other teachers embarrassed students to punish them. In some schools students who did not learn their lessons wore a dunce cap. The tall, pointed cap drew attention to the student. Some teachers also made the student sit on a stool in front of the class.

morals—beliefs about what is right and wrong

Chapter 4

SCHOOL DAYS

The school day started at sunrise. During fall and winter the schoolteacher started a fire in the stove early each morning. The teacher rang a hand bell, calling the children to class. As the students entered the building they "made their manners" to the teacher. Their morning greeting sometimes was followed by a bow from the boys and a **curtsy** from the girls.

A teacher and his students gather around the warm schoolhouse fire on a cold morning in 1880.

curtsy—to bend slightly at the knees, with one foot in front of the other

Teachers on the frontier designed school
lessons to give children a basic education in a
variety of subjects. Most schools taught reading,
writing, and arithmetic. Students also learned
religion, penmanship, composition, grammar,
spelling, and geography. Many schools offered
music, drawing, and singing lessons.

Schoolbooks were expensive. Some schools did not have enough for all of the students. Many schoolteachers taught lessons from personal books. Some teachers required students to bring a Bible from home. Most pioneer children studied from *McGuffey's Eclectic Readers* by William Holmes. The series of textbooks offered lessons for various grade levels. The *First Reader* was a primer, which taught young children to read through simple rhymes. Primer books also included lessons in the alphabet, spelling, and numbers. The *Second Reader* through the *Sixth Reader* included stories, famous speeches, and poems. The works taught students good morals. They encouraged hard work, honesty, **charity**, and proper manners.

78   MCGUFFEY'S FIRST READER

LESSON XLIV.

laid	lamb	where	fol-low
rule	what	fleece	ev-er-y
that	harm	school	wait-ed
love	made	ea-ger	ap-pear
sure	snow	Ma-ry	a-gainst
bind	white	gen-tle	an-i-mal
near	laugh	a-fraid	ling-er-ed
went	makes	teach-er	pa-tient-ly

MA-RY'S LAMB.

MA-RY had a lit-tle lamb,
  Its fleece was white as snow,
And ev-er-y where that Ma-ry went,
  The lamb was sure to go.

lesson from an 1853 edition of *McGuffey's First Eclectic Reader*

charity—to help someone in need

Readers also taught children proper penmanship. Students copied letters from their primers onto their slates. Some students practiced penmanship by writing essays in composition books.

In pioneer schools all children wrote with their right hand. If students tried writing with their left hand the teacher forced them to switch to hands. Some teachers tied students' left arms behind their backs to encourage them to use the "correct" hand.

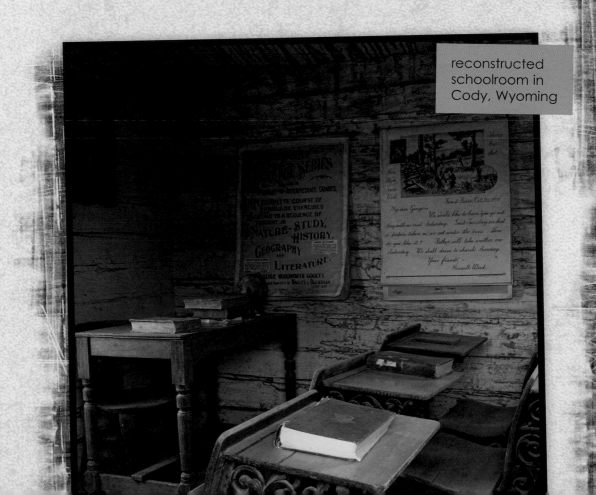

reconstructed schoolroom in Cody, Wyoming

Math Buzz

Number games such as Math Buzz strengthened students' multiplication skills. Schoolchildren sat in a circle and chose a buzz number. Each student began to count in turn. Whenever a student reached a multiple of the base number, the student said "buzz" instead of a number. For example, for the number three, the buzz count would be one, two, buzz, four, five, buzz, seven, eight, buzz . . . You can play Math Buzz with your friends. Choose different numbers to improve your multiplication skills.

Arithmetic drills improved students' problem-solving speed. The teacher wrote an arithmetic problem on the blackboard while the students solved it on their slates. Many teachers expected students to solve difficult problems in their heads. Pioneer students also memorized addition and multiplication tables.

Most frontier schools took breaks from classes throughout the day. Students took a lunch break over the noon hour. Most students brought lunches from home in metal or wooden buckets. After lunch students went outdoors for fresh air and exercise. Teachers also called a short recess in the morning and in the afternoon. The breaks allowed children to use the outhouse or to get a drink of water.

During recess most children played group games such as tag, hide-and-seek, and baseball. Many girls played games such as Cat's Cradle with long pieces of string tied together at the ends. Some girls played hopscotch or braided flower chains.

elementary students outside for recess

Chapter 5

SPELLING BEES AND EXAMINATIONS

Teachers invited the community to student activities and examinations. They spent the week before decorating the interior of the school.

Many frontier schools held spelling bees on Fridays or in the evenings. Pioneer children learned to spell from *Noah Webster's Elementary Spelling Book* and *McGuffey's Speller*. Students from opposing teams took turns spelling words the teacher chose.

Students spelled each word dividing it into syllables. For example, to spell *scarecrow*, the student spelled s-c-a-r-e, then said *scare*. Next, the student spelled c-r-o-w and said *crow*, *scarecrow*. After each correctly spelled word, students went to the end of their team's line. If students misspelled their words, they returned to their seats. The spelling bee continued until only one student remained standing.

Students line up in front of their teacher during a spelling bee.

During the Christmas season, frontier schools often organized a pageant. The evening program combined songs, poetry readings, and academic drills. A pageant often included a play. Students acted out familiar stories or wrote their own plays. The teachers invited the entire community to attend pageants.

Teachers tested the childrens' knowledge with end-of-term examinations. Many teachers held public examinations. Schoolchildren often recited poems and compositions. During examinations teachers judged the students' progress. Children who performed well could move to the next grade. Many students did not go to high school. Most students who did attend high school graduated when they were 15 or 16 years old. Teachers sometimes presented graduates with a decorated certificate.

After examinations the community often gathered for a picnic. Families brought food and played games at the community celebrations.

Many towns on the frontier continued to use one-room schoolhouses until the mid-1900s. As settlements grew people in frontier cities built public schools, academies, and colleges. By the early 1900s most children attended school on a regular basis.

A teacher gives an examination to his students.

MAKE A WRITING SLATE

African-American schools did not receive as much funding as white schools. Teachers often made their own school supplies.

What You Need

sandpaper
thin piece of plywood or craft
   wood, cut 8 by 12-inches
cloth rag

masking tape, 1-inch wide
newspapers
chalk spray paint
white or colored chalk
felt eraser

What You Do

1. Use the sandpaper to sand all the edges of the wooden board until it is smooth. Be careful of splinters. Lightly sand the top and bottom of the board.

2. Wipe all surfaces of the board with the rag to remove any loose sawdust.

3. Place strips of masking tape in a border along the outside edges of the board. Make sure the edge of the masking tape is flush with the edge of the board so the tape does not fold over the edge.

4. Spread two or three layers of newspaper on a firm surface. Place the board with the taped side up in the center of the paper.

5. With an adults help, lightly spray the surface of the wood with the chalk spray paint. Allow it to dry completely then apply a second coat. If paint appears thin in spots, spray additional coats. After each coat allow paint to dry completely.

6. Remove the masking tape from your slate.

GLOSSARY

charity (CHAYR-uh-tee)—to help someone in need

curtsy (KURT-see)—to bend slightly at the knees, with one foot in front of the other

donate (DOH-nayt)—to give something as a gift

drought (DROUT)—a long period of weather with little or no rainfall

hardship (HAHRD-ship)—something that causes suffering; usually hunger, and poverty

immigrant (IM-uh-gruhnt)—someone who moves from one country to live permanently in another

interfere (in-tur-FIHR)—to prevent for being carried out

morals (MOR-uhls)—beliefs about what is right and wrong

reservation (rez-ur-VAY-shuhn)—an area of land set aside for American Indians; in Canada reservations are called reserves

slate (SLAYT)—gray rock that can be split into thin layers

sod (SAHD)—a layer of soil with grass attached to it

tuition (too-ISH-uhn)—money paid to attend a school

veteran (VET-ur-uhn)—a person who served in the armed forces

READ MORE

Collins, Terry. *Into the West: Causes and Effects of U.S. Westward Expansion.* Cause and Effect. North Mankato, Minn.: Capstone Press, 2014.

Gunderson, Jessica. *Your Life as a Pioneer on the Oregon Trail.* The Way It Was. North Mankato, Minn.: Capstone Press, 2012.

Machajewski, Sarah. *A Kid's Life During the Westward Expansion.* How Kids Lived. New York: PowerKids Press, 2015.

INTERNET SITES

FactHound offers a safe, fun way to find Internet sites related to this book. All of the sites on FactHound have been researched by our staff.

Here's all you do:

Visit *www.facthound.com*

Type in this code: 9781515720966

 Check out projects, games and lots more at
www.capstonekids.com

CRITICAL THINKING USING THE COMMON CORE

1. What was the main goal of frontier schools? (Key Ideas and Details)

2. What happened to a student who tried to write with his or her left hand? (Key Ideas and Details)

3. Pioneer children often had end-of-year examinations. If they performed well, they moved on to the next grade level. How is this similar to school today? (Integration of Knowledge and Ideas)

INDEX